This book belongs to:

_____

In memory of my sweet Snoopy

PLEASE NOTE: This book contains twenty-four new hand-drawn illustrations; each picture appears twice. This provides the opportunity to use a different color scheme or different media on the second copy. Pages are printed on one side only, so that virtually any media may be used. It is recommended to insert a blotter paper beneath the page you are coloring.

SHARE YOUR CREATIONS!

Use #mysticallandschristmas on Instagram,
and visit www.instagram.com/mysticallandsart/
Visit us on Facebook at
www.facebook.com/mysticallandscoloringbook/

PLEASE FOLLOW MY
AUTHOR PAGE ON AMAZON!

Coloring Adventures in the Secret Realms

A Mystical Lands Christmas

Hand-drawn Pen and Ink Illustrations by

KAREN E. MYERS

Christmas Across the Mystical Lands

Christmas in the Mystical Lands is a time of heightened merriment and magic, a time for Yuletide celebrations and winter decorations. Explore little villages and secret hamlets, mushroom houses and tree stump cottages, all adorned for the joyful holiday festivities. Snowmen, Christmas trees, sleighs, gingerbread men, snowflakes, holly and ivy are waiting to be colored and magically brought to life!

So, relax, grab your favorite coloring supplies and a cup of hot cocoa, and prepare to enter an enchanted fantasy world, while leaving the stress and cares of the real world behind.

Throughout the Mystical Lands of Uchana, Kelswych and beyond, enjoy a magical journey in the Secret Realms during the most wonderful time of the year!

Happy Holidays!
Karen E. Myers

Color Test Page

❖

Experiment with color palettes here.

Advent Hall

Bamur
Bake Shop

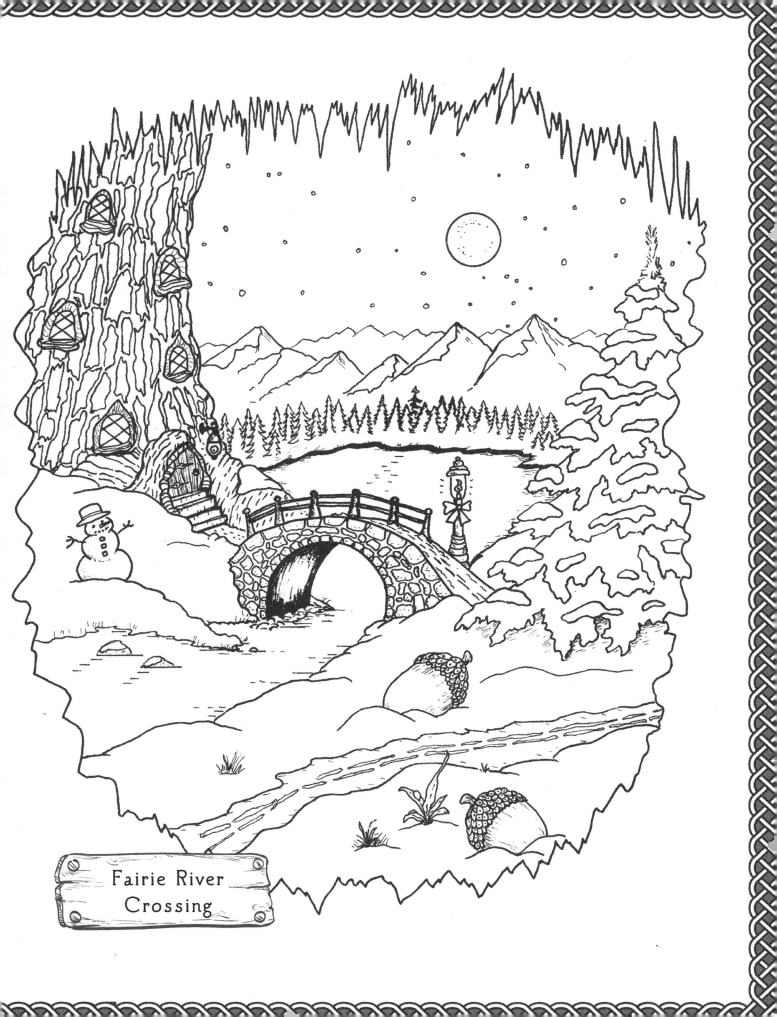

Fairie River
Crossing

Fairiefrost
Cottage

Festive Forest Hollow

Goodcheer
Guest House

Holiday Hamlet

Jolly Ridge
Snowfolke

Merry Mystic Cove

Mistletoe
Manor

Northwood
Noel

Pinecone
Grotto

Shadyside
Sleigh Ride

Snowdrop Inn

Snowflake Hollow

Snowvalley
Acres

Sugarbyrde
Chalet

Sugarplum
Shire

Trollmyre
Sweet Retreat

Winterchill
Cabin

Advent Hall

Bamur
Bake Shop

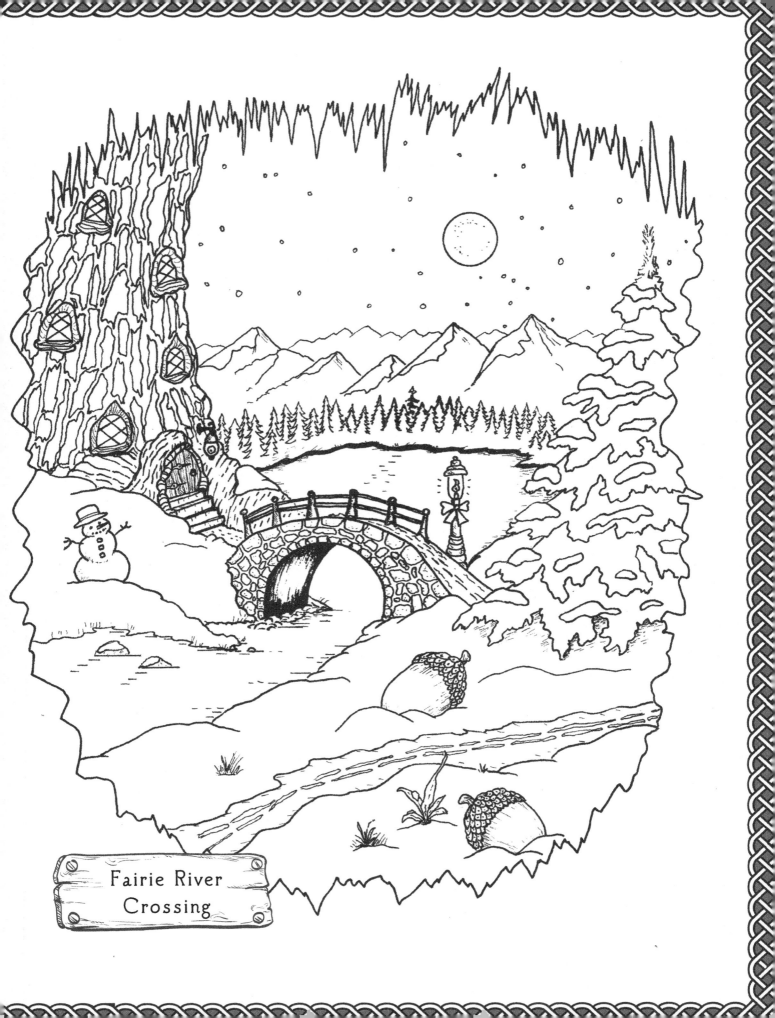

Fairie River
Crossing

Fairiefrost
Cottage

Festive Forest
Hollow

Goodcheer
Guest House

Holiday Hamlet

Jolly Ridge
Snowfolke

Merry Mystic Cove

Northwood
Noel

Pinecone
Grotto

Shadyside
Sleigh Ride

Snowdrop Inn

Snowvalley Acres

Sugarbyrde
Chalet

Sugarplum
Shire

Trollmyre
Sweet Retreat

Winterchill
Cabin

Yuletide
Hideaway

Made in the USA
Coppell, TX
09 February 2021